W9-BKL-763

POP'S BRIDGE

Written by EVE BUNTING
Illustrated by C. F. PAYNE

Harcourt, Inc.
Orlando Austin New York San Diego London
Printed in China

My pop is building the Golden Gate Bridge.

Almost every day after school, Charlie Shu and I go to Fort Point and watch. The bridge will stretch across the bay, from San Francisco to Marin. People said this bridge couldn't be built. Some call it the impossible bridge. They say the bay is too deep, the currents too strong, the winds blowing in from the ocean too fierce.

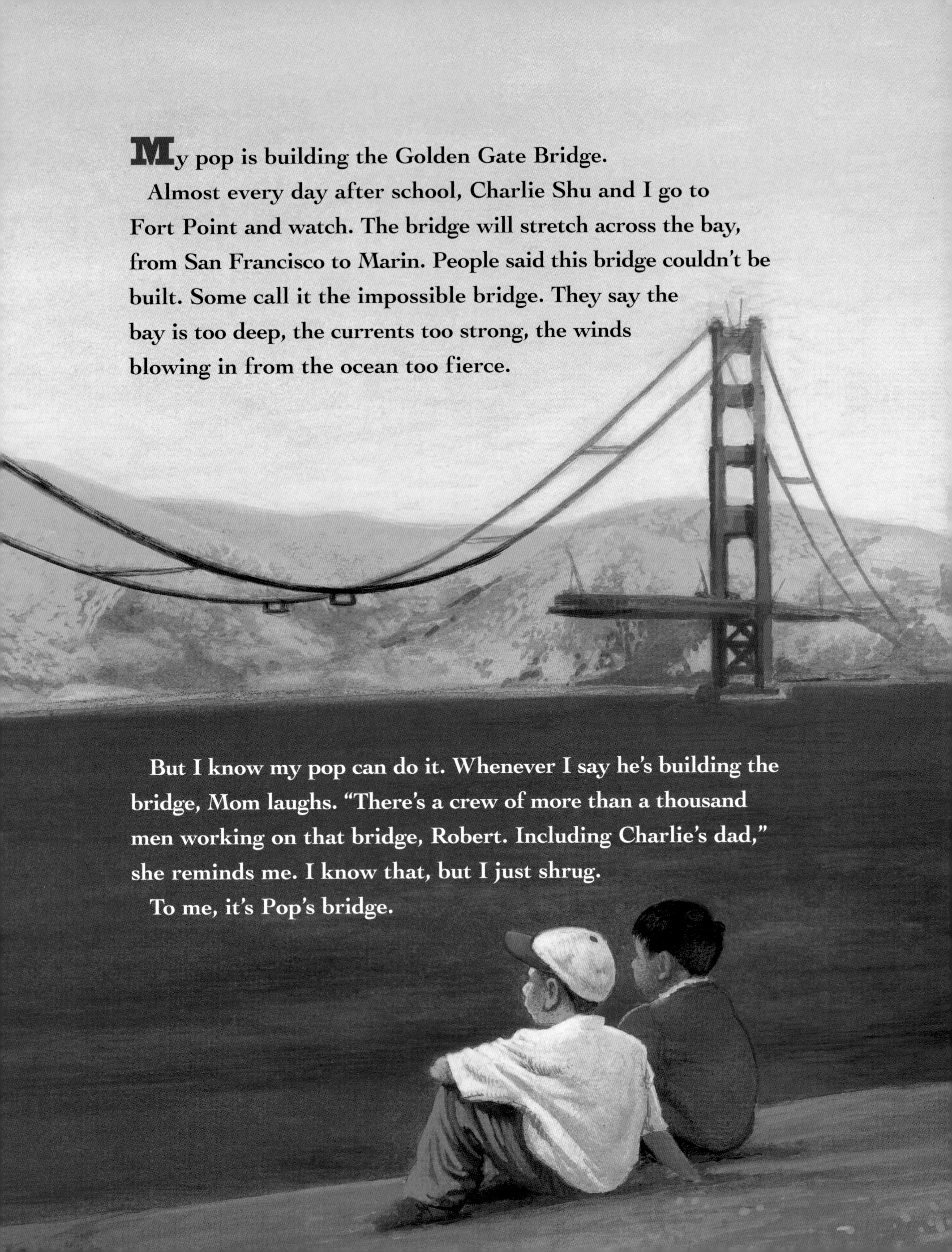

But I know my pop can do it. Whenever I say he's building the bridge, Mom laughs. "There's a crew of more than a thousand men working on that bridge, Robert. Including Charlie's dad," she reminds me. I know that, but I just shrug.

To me, it's Pop's bridge.

Pop's a high-iron man, balancing on the slatted catwalks, spinning and bending the cables. He climbs so high that sometimes clouds come down around his shoulders. When the fog rolls in, he disappears completely. That's why the high-iron men are called skywalkers.

Charlie's dad is a painter. The painters start work long before the bridge is even finished. My pop says if it weren't for them, the bridge would rust away, but I think he's just saying that to be nice. The skywalkers have the most important job of all.

At Fort Point I look for Pop through the binoculars Mom lends me. The workers look alike in their overalls and swabbie hats, but I can always find my pop because of the red kerchief he ties at his throat. It's our own scarlet signal.

I don't worry much about him on days when the sun sparkles on the water, when sailboats skim below. It's so beautiful I can forget that it's dangerous, too. But when the wind blows through the Golden Gate, the men cling to the girders like caterpillars on a branch. On foggy days my hands sweat on the binoculars. *Where is he?* When I find him, I try not to look away, as though the force of my eyes can keep him from falling.

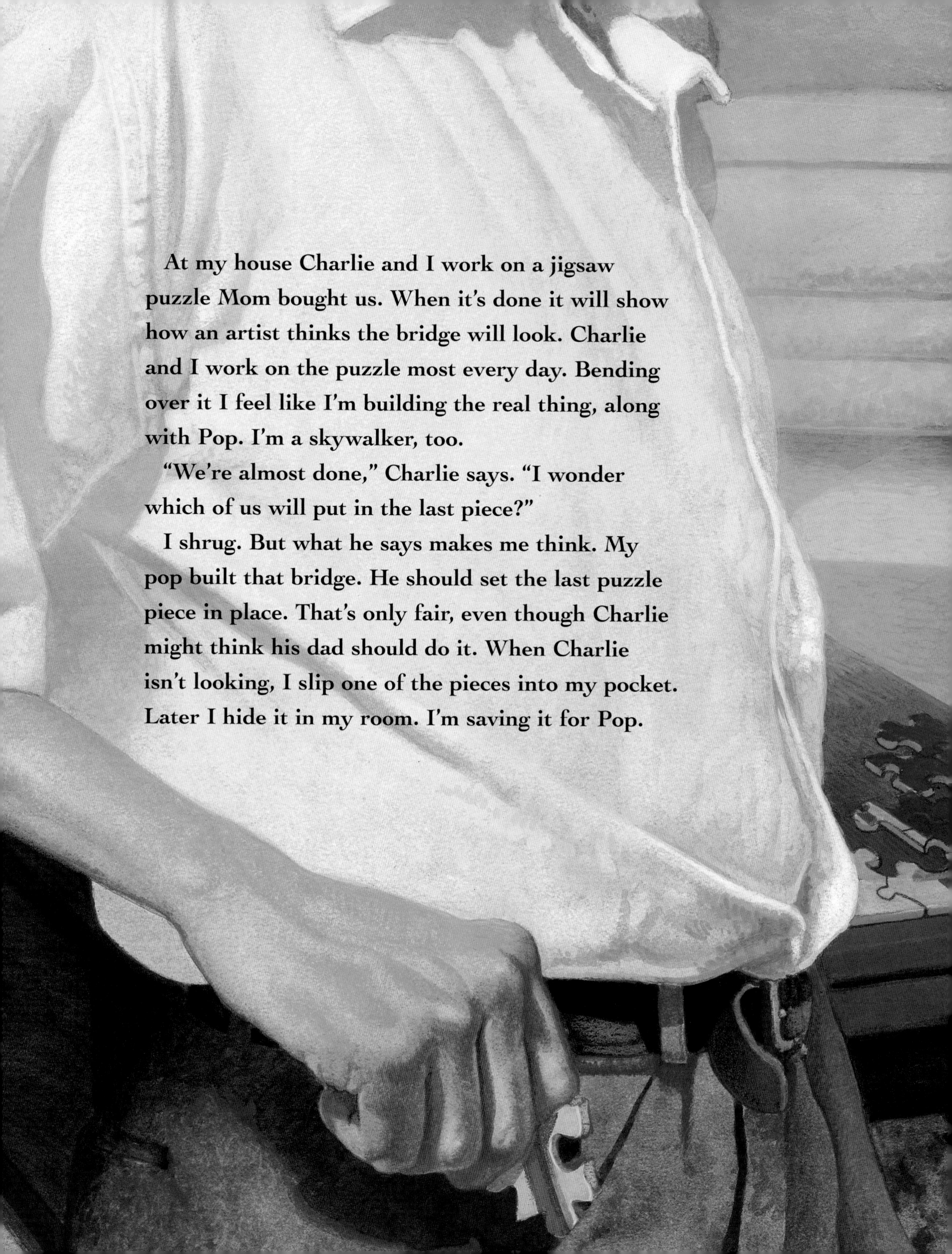

At my house Charlie and I work on a jigsaw puzzle Mom bought us. When it's done it will show how an artist thinks the bridge will look. Charlie and I work on the puzzle most every day. Bending over it I feel like I'm building the real thing, along with Pop. I'm a skywalker, too.

"We're almost done," Charlie says. "I wonder which of us will put in the last piece?"

I shrug. But what he says makes me think. My pop built that bridge. He should set the last puzzle piece in place. That's only fair, even though Charlie might think his dad should do it. When Charlie isn't looking, I slip one of the pieces into my pocket. Later I hide it in my room. I'm saving it for Pop.

The "impossible bridge" is nearly finished. One evening Mom and Pop and I walk down to Fort Point. The bridge hangs between stars and sea.

"It's like a giant harp," my pop says. "A harp for the angels to play." I look up at him, and I can tell this wasn't just a job to my pop. He loves the bridge.

In San Francisco there is great excitement. Everyone is waiting for opening day.

Charlie and I have watched nearly every bit of the bridge go up. We saw the two spans come together from opposite directions. We saw them meet. We saw the roadway go in. And my pop did it. No one can be as proud as I am. Not even Charlie. After all, my dad is a skywalker.

BRIDGE COMPLE

And then one day, something terrible happens. Charlie and I are watching as the scaffolding pulls away from the bridge. There's a noise like a train wreck as the scaffolding crashes down into the safety net. The net tears loose, and men go with it into the swirling tide.

I can't breathe. I can't think.

But then I look hard through the binoculars and see Pop still on the bridge, his red kerchief whipping. "Pop!" I whisper in relief. Beside me Charlie is screaming, "Where's my dad? Where's my dad?"

We had seen him working close to that scaffolding. I can't see him now.

“We’ll find him,” I promise. “We have to.” I sweep the binoculars up and down the bridge cables, looking at every painter hanging high on his Jacob’s ladder or swinging in a bosun’s chair, like a knot on a rope.

“Be there, Mr. Shu,” I plead, and then I spot him. “Over by that cross girder!” I yell. Charlie fumbles for the binoculars. I help him. He looks where I point.

“He’s there! He’s safe!” Charlie gasps.

The next day we find out that only two of the twelve men in the water were saved.

I think and think about that day. At night, half asleep, I see the bridge shake. I hear the crash. One of those men in the water could have been Pop. Or Charlie's dad.

I finally understand, and I feel ashamed. Equal work, equal danger, for skywalkers *and* for painters.

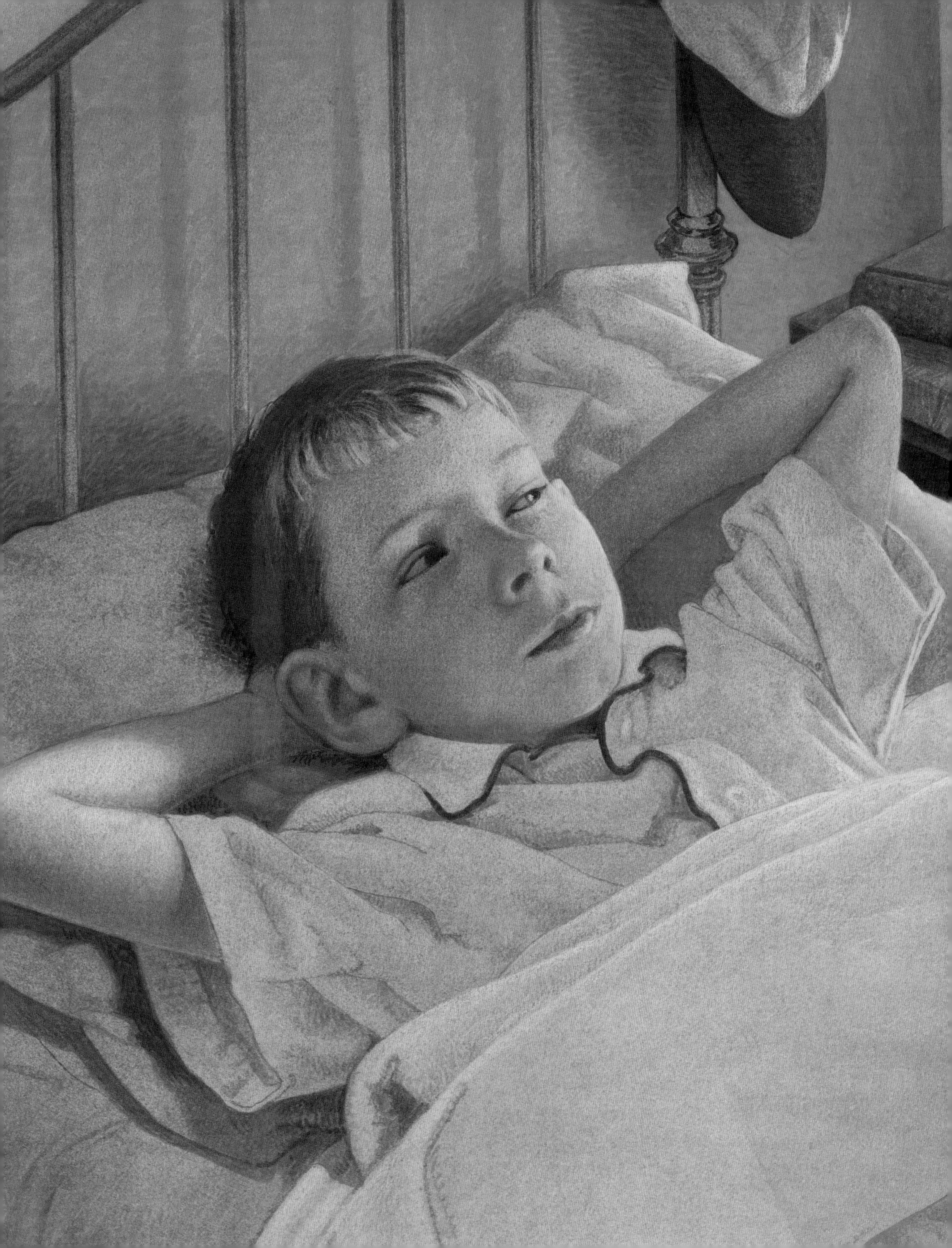

The work goes on. A new safety net is put in place. Pop says there's less talking and joking now among the men. There's a remembering.

But the bridge must be finished. And at last it is. We watch through Mom's binoculars as the golden spike is drilled in at the center of the main span. Now the celebration can begin.

On opening day no cars are allowed. Thousands of people walk and dance and roller-skate across the bridge, including us. I wear Pop's kerchief around my neck. There's a man riding a unicycle. There's another on stilts. Navy biplanes fly above the great steel towers. Battleships and cruisers sail below the bridge and into San Francisco Bay. Wind strums its music through the stretch of the cables, and I think of my pop's harp.

That night our family has our own party with Charlie and his dad. There's stewed chicken and a Chinese noodle dish Charlie's dad made and a snickerdoodle pie.

The jigsaw puzzle sits on the coffee table with a gap in the middle. "I've searched and searched for that missing piece," my mother says.

"A good thing we didn't leave our bridge with a space like that," Mr. Shu says.

Pop chuckles. "We'd be working still."

It's time.

I slip upstairs to get the hidden puzzle piece, then find the scissors and cut the piece carefully in half. I go back down and put a half piece in Mr. Shu's hand and the other in my pop's. "Finish it," I say. "It's your bridge. It belongs to both of you."

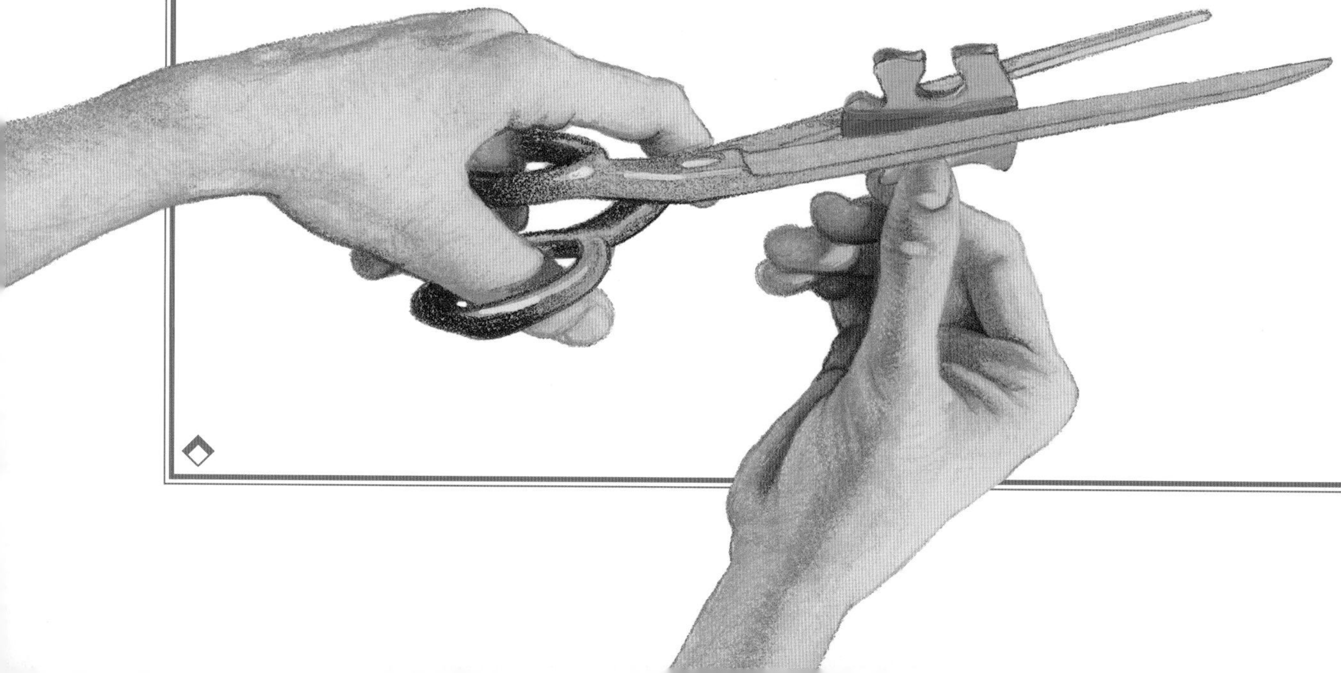

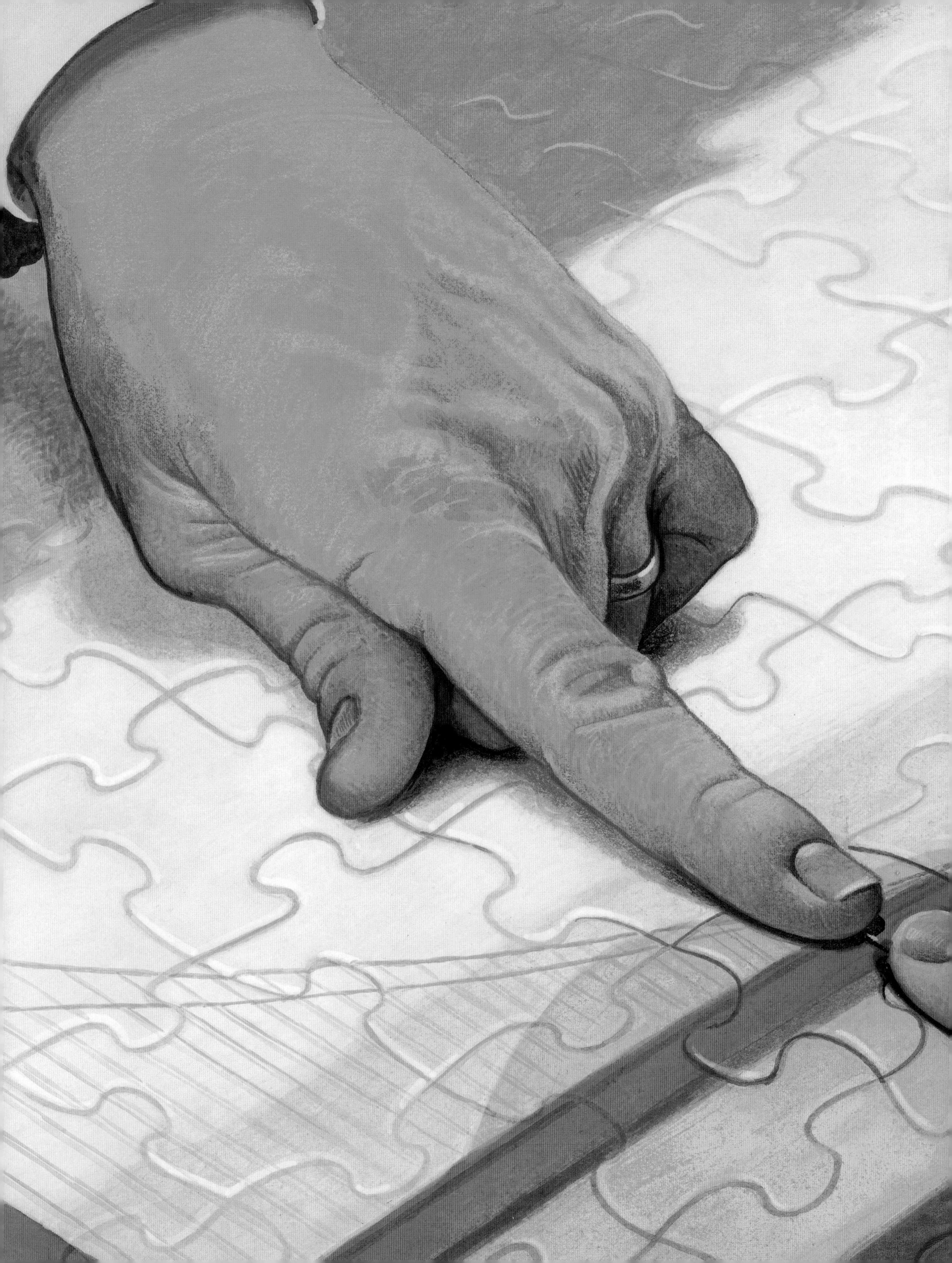

My mother raises her eyebrows and Charlie says, "Hey, where . . . ?" But I just watch as the two pieces fit in, so perfectly, so smoothly.

"Team effort," my pop says.

We raise our glasses of sarsaparilla to celebrate the laborers and riveters, the carpenters and the painters and the skywalkers. All the men who worked together to build the most beautiful bridge in the world.

A Note from the Author

The Golden Gate is the stretch of water between San Francisco and Marin County in California. Before 1933 the only way to cross this part of the San Francisco Bay was by ferry. A bridge was needed.

But how could one be built? The span is more than a mile wide. The water is deep and treacherous, with strong tides rushing in and out of the Golden Gate each day. Winds of up to eighty miles per hour roar in from the Pacific Ocean and can churn up fifty-foot waves. What bridge could be long enough and strong enough to overcome these obstacles? And what would happen to the bridge and to the traffic on it if an earthquake hit? The terrible 1906 San Francisco earthquake was still a recent memory.

An engineer named Joseph Baermann Strauss claimed that a suspension bridge could be built and that he was the man to build it. He estimated the cost would be $35 million. That was another obstacle. Where would the money come from?

Despite his many critics, Joseph Strauss was unshakeable. He drew up the plans. He persisted. He had the know-how. And in the end, people listened and believed.

The money was raised by taxes and the sale of bonds. Strauss agreed that if bids for construction costs went above his estimate, the deal was off. He knew the dream that he'd worked on for years was close to becoming a reality.

Jobs for laborers on the bridge went only to local workers. More than a thousand men worked on the bridge from its beginning in January 1933 to its completion in April 1937. Some lost their lives. Although Robert, Charlie, and their families are fictional, the tragic accident in this story really happened.

The suspension bridge was flexible enough to survive the force of the winds. Its great towers and cables were strong enough to carry the traffic that would cross its roadway. It was limber enough so the towers would sway without breaking and the cables would stretch without snapping if there was an earthquake. A quake did jolt the bridge during construction. One of the towers swayed sixteen feet toward the ocean and sixteen feet back toward the bay. It righted itself and remained secure and standing.

When the Golden Gate Bridge was finished, there was more than a million dollars left over. What a triumph! In May 1937, the "impossible bridge" was finally open. The city of San Francisco—and the world—celebrated.

Less than a year later, Joseph Baermann Strauss, the man everyone called the practical dreamer, died. He had once been asked how long he expected his beautiful bridge to last. Confidently he'd replied, "Forever."

For all those who worked to build
the most beautiful bridge in the world
—E. B.

For my dad
—C. F. P.

For information about permission to reproduce selections from this book, please write Permissions, Houghton Mifflin Harcourt Publishing Company
215 Park Avenue South NY NY 10003.

www.hmhbooks.com

Library of Congress Cataloging-in-Publication Data
Bunting, Eve, 1928–
Pop's bridge/Eve Bunting; illustrated by C. F. Payne.
p. cm.
Summary: Robert and his friend Charlie are proud of their fathers who are working on the construction of San Francisco's Golden Gate Bridge.
1. Golden Gate Bridge (San Francisco, Calif.)—Juvenile fiction. [1. Golden Gate Bridge (San Francisco, Calif.)—Fiction. 2. Bridges—Design and construction—Fiction. 3. Fathers—Fiction. 4. San Francisco (Calif.)—History—20th century—Fiction.] I. Payne, C. F., ill. II. Title.
PZ7.B91527Pob 2006
[E]—dc22 2004023774
ISBN-13: 978-0-15-204773-3 ISBN-10: 0-15-204773-5

SCP 8
4500438244

The illustrations in this book were done in mixed media
on cold press illustration board.
The display type was set in OptiEgiziano.
The text type was set in Cochin.
Color separations by Bright Arts Limited, Hong Kong
Printed in China by RR Donnelley
Production supervision by Pascha Gerlinger
Designed by Lydia D'moch